e Flying Bath

For Felix – J.D.
For Christine Isteed – D.R.

First published 2014 by Macmillan Children's Books

This edition published 2015 by Macmillan Children's Books

an imprint of Pan Macmillan, a division of

Macmillan Publishers Limited

20 New Wharf Road, London N1 9RR

Associated companies throughout the world

www.panmacmillan.com

ISBN: 978-1-4472-7711-8

Text copyright © Julia Donaldson 2014

Illustrations copyright © David Roberts 2014

Moral rights asserted.

1 3 5 7 9 8 6 4 2

A CIP catalogue record for this book is available from the British Library.

Printed in China

WRITTEN BY
JULIA DONALDSON

ILLUSTRATED BY
DAVID ROBERTS

The Flying Bath

MACMILLAN CHILDREN'S BOOKS

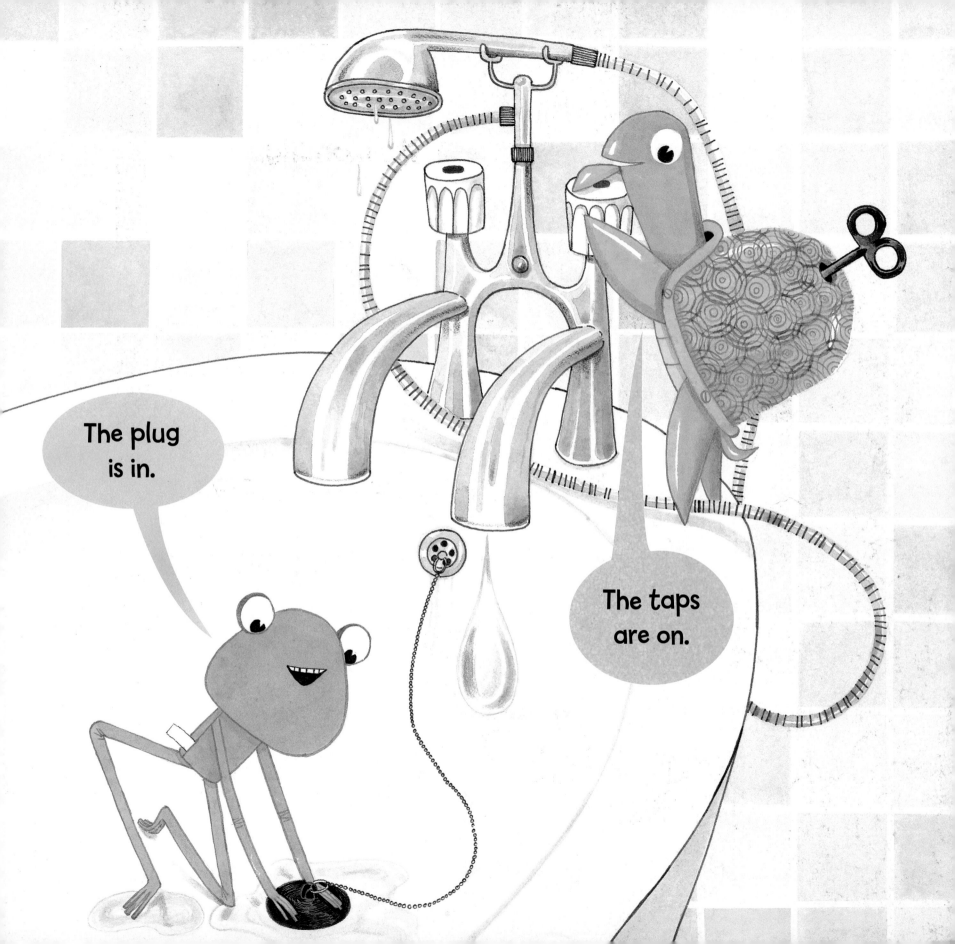

Wings out, and off we fly.
The Flying Bath is in the sky!

Wings out, and off we fly.
The Flying Bath is in the sky!

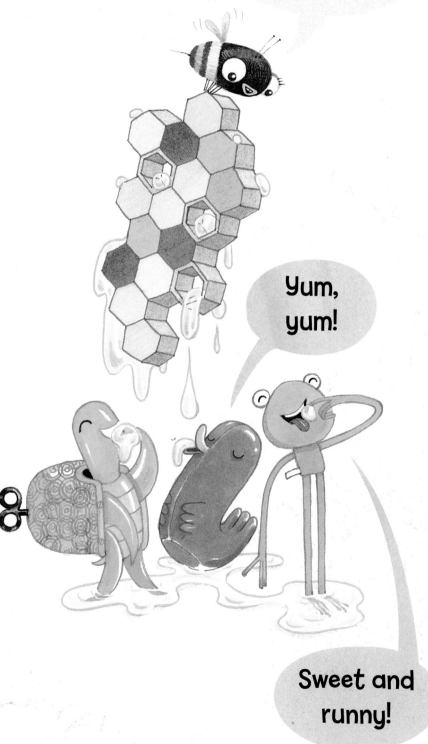

Wings out, and off we fly.
The Flying Bath is in the sky!

Thank you. Shall we all play tig?

Faster, faster!

Got you, Pig!

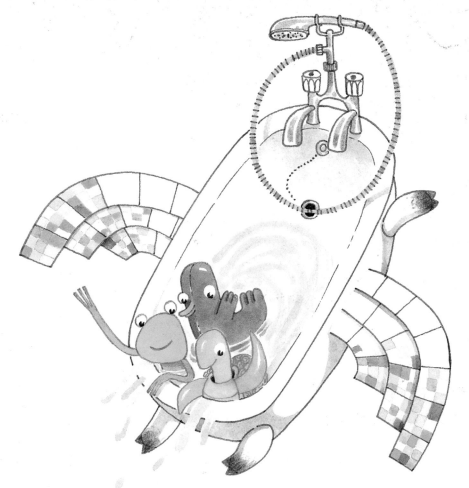

Wings out, and off we fly.
The Flying Bath is in the sky!

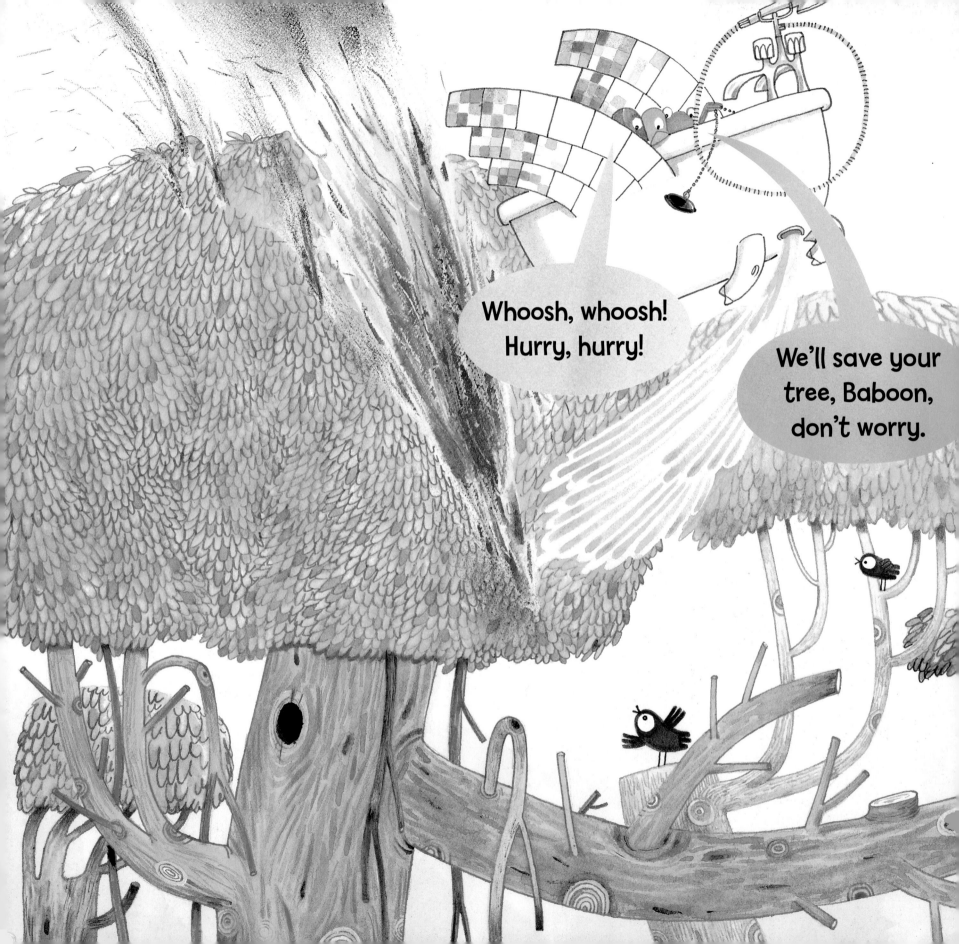

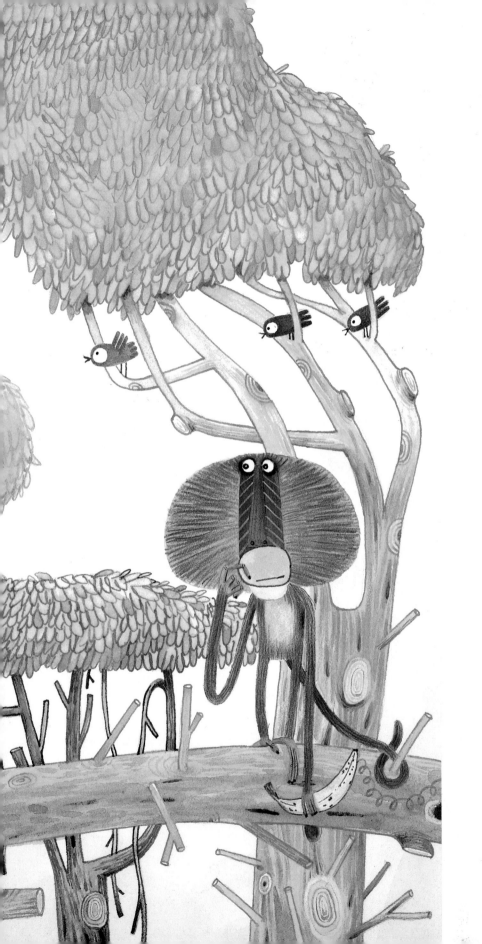

A fish is frantic.
There's a drought.
He says his pond
is drying out.

Wings out, and off we fly.
The Flying Bath is in the sky!

... but now it's late.
The Flying Bath has got a date.

Wings out, and off we fly.
The Flying Bath is in the sky!